COUNT DRACULA AND THE GHOST

One night, Count Dracula opened
his coffin and looked out.
"No one here as usual," he moaned.
"Night after night all on my own."

Count Dracula flew round his castle.
"No one here.
I'll have to be on my own tonight
as usual. It's not fair.

I need victims, but night after night
I'm on my own."

Then there was a knock at the door.

"A victim," shouted the Count.
"Tonight I'll not be on my own
after all.
A victim has come to my castle.
A victim is knocking at my door."

Knock! Knock!
"I'm coming," shouted the Count.
"Don't worry, I'm coming."
He flew downstairs to
open the door.

Count Dracula opened the door and
looked out.
"Come in, come in!
Welcome to my castle."

Count Dracula looked out into the night.
"No one here," he moaned.
"There was a knock, knock, knock
on my door, but there is no one here.
It's not fair.
No victim after all.
All on my own again."

8

Out of the night came a voice.
"Count Dracula, I'm here.
Can I come into your castle?"

"Come out," shouted the Count.
"I can't see you."

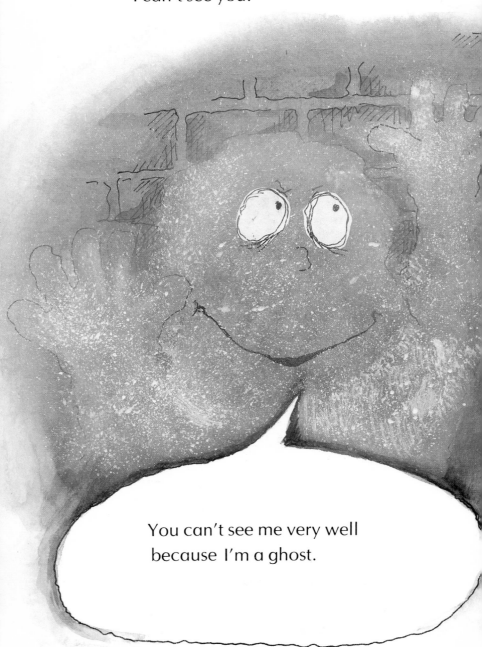

You can't see me very well
because I'm a ghost.

"A ghost?" shouted the Count.
A ghost can't be a victim.
A ghost has no blood.
Oh no! What a disappointment."

"I need a home," said the ghost.
"And I need a castle to haunt."
"This can't be your home,"
shouted the Count.

But you are all on your own.
If I haunt your castle you won't be on
your own night after night.

I'll be here.
You'll like that.

"If I let you haunt my castle,"
said the Count,
"will you help me find victims to bite?"
"All right," said the ghost.
"I need victims too.
Victims to scare.
We will find victims together."

"Ha ha! You are not such a disappointment after all," said the Count. "You can haunt my castle. That's a fair deal."

The Count and the ghost sat down together.
"Let us drink," shouted the Count.
"To victims and lots of them."